MW00713406

Little Data

Christopher Schaberg & Mark Yakich

RED FLAG PRESS

USE YOUR WORDS

Little Data

Contents

for
Owen, Samara, Julien, Camille, Jonah, and Vera

Acorn

The average three-year-old can hold no more than 11 acorns in both hands before they begin to fall onto the sidewalk, each small *ka-thunk* eliciting screams from the child and proximate blue jays in kind.

The animated film *My Neighbor Totoro* hinges on acorns: as treasure, hope, gift, loss, and life. For the two little girls in the movie, acorns are portals to an alternative world, one which exists right outside their screen door.

It will always break a small part of your heart to pull up the volunteer baby live oaks whose subterranean acorns have germinated against all odds in your backyard. As the years pass by, you will grow to understand that it is precisely those small parts of your heart that are the most concerning.

Advice

How many nuggets of advice can the average human brain hold?

No one has done the research—yet—but theoretically the number is ungraspable. Which is perhaps why advice, whether from Mom and Dad or the Nobel Laureate in Economics or the latest parenting website, seems so relentless.

Studies show, however, that as soon as a statistic is published it is, by definition, already outdated. That is simply a function of contemporary living—and living by science. Today's version of 1950s "Better Living through Chemistry" may be "Better Living through Algorithms."

While data-driven analysis is often useful, if not crucial, to improving the lives of *Homo sapiens*, not least of all their offspring (cf. infant mortality rates), the data—so much, so big—just as often is rendered ineffectual in the face of a screaming toddler or a graduating senior who you could swear was just the other day that toddler. Algorithms fall apart in the presence of a truculent child. Parenting advice is never a silver bullet. It's more like a paper plane in nosedive.

While it can't be proven, most people only ever take half of the advice they are given. And of advice taken, only half of that will turn out to have been good advice. As for giving advice to your teenager, the less proffered the better.

Airports

An increasing number of airports around the world feature dedicated children's play areas, including jungle gyms, imitation airplane fuselages, simulacral cottages, and gigantic, child-body-scale chess boards.

Let us assume that 50% of airports take child play into consideration through the planning and design phases all the way to construction. Meanwhile, 100% of airports *are* de facto already a child's playground: seats to climb on, floors to slide across, escalators to disobey, trams to ride, and overhead announcements to mimic.

No one likes being in an airport with screaming children. But neither does one necessarily like to see children making fun out of the whole experience. Which is worse, your child playing hide-and-seek in the food court, or chicken fried rice regurgitated in the midst of a crying fit?

There comes a time to decide: Do you join in the child play, misuse the space in glee—or scold your children as you wait out the delay?

Algorithms

Every year more romantic relationships are facilitated by algorithmic pairing. And why not?

Algorithm is simply a fancy term (if sometimes hard to spell) for *doing the math*. It comes from *algorismus*, a Medieval Latin word that sounds like the name of a small dinosaur, but is actually a butchered transliteration of an Arabic word for "native of Khawrazm." This is just what Wikipedia says. It could be all lies. Then again, whenever someone says "you can't trust" Wikipedia, they are usually misinformed and untrustworthy.

To the point: algorithms make things go. They make things work. They stack, they queue. They merge-sort and quick-sort and heap-sort.

They make things make sense. Breadth first, or depth first?

They can be run. They can deliver results. When in doubt, flood fill.

They are incontrovertible. Plug them in. Read what comes out.

Insert, search, delete.

Be amazed at how they predict your taste. You are most definitely yourself! The algorithms will prove it. And your children are, it turns out, children by the books.

Is our behavior algorithmically predictable, or do the algorithms that declare our behavior is predictable create predictability? This is not a word game.

Or it is a word game, but most people are paying more attention to the numbers than to the words.

Amazon

No longer a river, but a portal. Or a floodgate. The trickle turned to an endless stream of junk you don't need—but was such a good deal! Children's flatware made of compostable something or other. Sound machines for sound sleep that never arrives. Six-packs of Halloween-themed underpants. All delivered in two days for free!

Free?

At the end of the day…it's simply the end of the day. But what to do with all the cardboard and bubble wrap? Don't throw it out. Recycle it. (Though beware of following the recycling truck to its terminus, out of curiosity. That journey may not end well.)

If you are lucky, what you order today will become one of the 33 million packages that will be pirated from doorways, porches, and welcome mats this year.

Ancestry

DNA results say 1.3% Neanderthal, and a high probability of distinctive odor from urine after eating asparagus. Did Neanderthals eat asparagus? Maybe some springs that's all they had to eat. Fresh out of the ground, less than a centimeter in diameter, there is nothing more scrumptious than wild asparagus. Asparagus is 93% water but 100% delicious. The fact that it can make your pee smell is complicated, as this also has something to do with different people's olfactory receptors, or so you've heard from a friend with quite different DNA than you.

No matter how much you know about where you came from, none of this will be of use when you are staring down the next generation in a fierce battle of wills. You ask her to pee before bed, and she insists she doesn't need to. He wants to wipe his own bottom, and you insist you still need to help. The skirmishes escalate. Toilet paper is torn, tears are shed. All for what? So that you can proclaim your rightful place in an ancestral line? Instead, you have planted a little seed of hatred that will grow like asparagus. When it flowers it will look nothing like it did when you might have harvested it. The next year, parched, skeletal, and golden, it'll look different once again.

Anecdote

In a relatively wealthy district in Connecticut, four leading education experts devised a method for crunching the data of every single public school student in the county, in order to produce daily individualized learning plans for an entire academic year. The results were off the charts. Each grade outperformed their highest performing peers across the state, indeed across the country. Baselines were elevated and goalposts narrowed. Test scores soared across the board. A happiness consultant measured significant increases at every level.

Unfortunately, as a success story it was judged as precisely that: a story. The methodology could not be implemented at scale, due to the outcome having been interpreted as anecdotal evidence first and foremost. The effort was considered an anomaly. Peer reviewers found fault with the rubrics and metrics involved in the project, and the conclusions were deemed fuzzy at best.

Each student was still provided with a badge for participating in what was colloquially referred to (with not a small amount of pride) as "the great little data crunch experiment." From that cohort, five graduates of the school district currently serve as leaders of major technology companies. Two others are being held in maximum-security prisons in undisclosed locations. The majority of the badge-earners live among us, blending in, existing as if they are normal.

Authority

"You're not the boss of me!" The daily, fragile pretext of who is in charge, who makes the rules, who breaks them, who breaks down. Then to start it all over again.

Am I even the boss of myself?

The question will haunt you.

Either way, nine out of ten bosses end up being assholes.

Does your spouse ever refer to you, directly or privately, as "the management"? Are you *that* asshole?

Backpack

Like a little evening dress people want to be seen in, or want to slip off someone else, there is the ubiquitous backpack—a metaphor for nothing but itself. Brand new, they smell amazing. After a few weeks at school—putrid.

For a parent of a child heading back to school in the U.S., the practical question is: *Should I get the bulletproof one?*

The bulletproof backpack is only so bulletproof. It can withstand the bullet of a 9mm handgun but not that of a .45 not to mention an AR-15 or AK-47. Technically, a bulletproof backpack is called *bullet resistant*, or more truthfully, call it a *bullseye.*

It might be better to buy the new bulletproof hoodie, called the Wonder Hoodie. But a hoodie can't hold your homework or lunch, only cover your head and heart.

Leave the backpack by the front door or by your bedside? Leave it when the active shooter bursts through the door, or cling to it for dear life?

Before bedtime-capitalism requires such difficult choices. But a dream, yes, it requires society.

Bathtime

To buy the baby shampoo, the bubble bath, the salt bomb.

To bathe with a child and pretend one is at the bottom of the sea. To have one's hair run through with a lice comb by a kindergartener until the scalp is scraped raw. To enjoy it more than anything else in the day. Until a small poop floats to the top, bobbing along with the bubbles. To enjoy that, too.

For the average American child, bathtime lasts 12 minutes. And the median size of a bubble is the size of a human eyeball. As for humans, about 801,000 of them younger than five years of age die from diarrhea each year, the vast majority due to unsafe drinking water.

Beach

There is no simpler place for a parent and child than the beach, where the horizon serves to humble, and the waves temper the dynamic between two souls with an abundance of life and an expanse of shoreline. Nothing could be easier than parenting in this moment. Stones and shells are collected, gulls remark happily on the scene from above. But then the child drinks sea water or throws a rock that hits you in the gut or the back of the head; a rotting fish is stepped on; lost balloon strings spill from the sand. The child cries, is hungry or tired. There's sand in the sandwich bread. Everyone is sunburnt. It's an impossible walk back to the car. Fuck the beach. There are more molecules in one drop of water than there are grains of sand on Earth.

Beatings

The kids punch and pinch and sometimes bite each other. If one could only allow them to do it without intervention, without worry that one of them will get seriously hurt and there will be a trip to the ER.... Maybe just once, to see how far it goes. A Fight Club for kids, with rules and clear guidelines. But it never happens because one of them will always run to you screaming bloody murder. *He started it. No, she started it. No, they started it.* It's a creation story: *In the beginning, someone started beating someone else. There was blood. And there were tears....* Would there eventually be forgiveness? And how do you forgive someone who will never ask for it?

Best Friends

At first they will get in the way. For many years they will obstruct your patterns, ruin your oldest friendships, and compromise your hard-earned sense of adulthood. Instead of Rage Against the Machine, you'll find yourself listening to Raffi's Lullabies: The Best Of. Almost all date nights will turn into prune juice: a child is constipated, you are anxious.

But one day they begin singing along to David Bowie. Games of hide-and-seek become sublime adventures. Bedtime is suddenly a new sacred ritual, even if they mostly sleep between you and your partner in the conjugal bed.

Admit it: the children have turned into your best friends.

Someday they will make other best friends, and even BFFs who will replace you. Have no fear. There is no such thing as *forever*: only endless blips and drips, a stream of little data flowing.

Books

People don't read books anymore—you hear that a lot. And yet, according to the numbers, more books are being sold each year than ever, and more bookshops are popping up everywhere.

The children ask to go to the library every weekend. They discover graphic novels, and in the "Teen" section of the library graphic novels that are, in fact, graphic. And the "I Survived…" books, which they devour. 9/11. The Nazi Invasion (they pronounce it *nah-zee*). The sinking of the *Titanic*. As long as they're reading, right?

In order to read you need quiet. You demand it, cry for it even, against the din of parading children after dinner. The stainless steel mixing bowl has become a drum keeping rhythm to your madness. Later in bed you relish it; you can read a novel. You can audibly track the full arc of an Airbus on final descent, from far horizon to reverse thrust upon landing. Later still you will wake up from a novel-triggered nightmare (it is called *The Anomaly*, a mind-bender replete with a Boeing 787 and multiversal travel). Lying there you will think about your job and all the goals you need to set, the deadlines you need to meet, the deliverables you haven't yet delivered. You'll picture your feckless manager at his cluttered desk, and all you want is for the quiet to end, for your children to be climbing loudly over you, for your book to clatter to the ground.

Boredom

"I'm bored." This becomes something between a mantra and a whine. You try to explain how boredom is a gift, a fascinating temporality in which to linger, if not to plunge. To which the response is, "I'm bored."

Everywhere boredom looms. After dinner, on the weekends, during the crosstown drive to school, at the bus stop, in line at the grocery store for Christ's sake. "I'm bored." That phrase clings to almost everything, like tendrils of a creeping vine whose roots seem impossible to locate, much less unearth.

You want to scream *Life is boring! Get used to it!* Instead you suggest I-spy, storytelling, or picture drawing. You attempt to invoke David Foster Wallace: *boring* means *tunneling in*, too. Do you feel it, the magic?

"I'm bored!"

You feel that vein in the left side of your neck start to pulse again. You mentally count to ten. You decide to offer to build a marble machine, or make a maze out of blocks.

But precisely at that moment, they're gone. They've found something to do. They don't need you. It's *you* who are boring. And isn't that one of the reasons you had them in the first place—because you were bored of yourself?

When Gautama was in the jungle during his spiritual awakening, he was allegedly never bored even though he was afraid. It is unclear whether the Buddha would be afraid of boredom, were he to meet it on the street.

Car

You back it up near the house so that the three linked extension cords will allow the vacuum to reach.

Open the doors, pull out the floor mats. Face the shallows of pretzel crumbs and tangerine peels, popcorn and rice cake shoals. Reckon with raisin amalgams gobbed in between seatbelt recesses. Traverse actual dunes of sand. Gather pebbles of all sorts, a veritable geological survey. Collect crumpled tissues containing calcified green snot. Scoop up scraps of paper, receipts and doodles, cupcake cups and lollipop wrappers. Assemble the apple cores, peach pits, pistachios, and almond slivers shorn from the tops of long-gone croissants.

This is the record of your daily schlepps to school, running errands, going to birthday parties. It is hard to overstate how good it feels to suck up or otherwise remove this accumulation, to bring the floors and seats of the vehicle back to something approximating clean.

The next morning, you decide to initiate a new policy which the owner of the car wash recommended: only water and celery are allowed to be consumed in the car.

"Celery?" the oldest child says. "Why not carrot sticks?"

"They stain. Celery doesn't make crumbs."

The three-year-old thinks this over, then says, "But we don't have celery. We'll have to get some at the store!"

He is your new favorite child.

Cheese Stick

An edible sword innocently wielded by a toddler. After an hour in a hot car, a limp, condomed phallus. Those are the white ones. Mozzarella. There are no words for the orange rectilinear cheddar versions, even if some children seem to live on them as their chief source of protein.

The origins of string cheese, cheese stick's progenitor, are debatable. In Mexico, a 14-year-old named Leobarda is credited with inventing string cheese in 1885. In Slovakia, there is a history of smoked and unsmoked string cheese, *korbáčiky*, made of sheep's milk and braided like little girls' hair.

Let the debate go. There is no doubt that when mozzarella is warmed to 140° F and stretched, the milk proteins line up perfectly.

Climbing

You planted a willow in the backyard when the sapling was the diameter of your thumb.

"Let me ask you a question, Papa. What do the skeletons of trees look like?" You tell him the story of the burned mountainside in Montana you once hiked, charred remains of lodgepole pines standing tombstone-like. But now you think perhaps they looked more skeletal. You were looking for morels, but before you get to the mushroom part of the story, your son is already bored.

Now the willow's trunk is thicker than you and your wife locked in an embrace.

The children discover the willow is climbable. They scale its branches nearly to the swaying top. The delight of trees, the simple fact of leaves and green. They have never been happier.

Your reverie is shattered when you hear a shriek from outside, and watch your son limping back toward the house. Sooner or later they always fall.

Coffee

Should I kill myself or just have another cup of coffee? That's what the great existentialist Albert Camus asked himself many mornings.

At least allegedly. The only proof is an uncited mention in *The Paradox of Choice* by Barry Schwartz, a book that "explains why too much of a good thing has proven detrimental to our psychological and emotional well-being."

What precisely is the opportunity cost of buying that zarfed cardboard cup of coffee instead of x, y, or z?

Two bucks—according to the self-proclaimed Coffee Detective and the gentleman who runs a site called Tough Nickel. The test kitchen says that one can make a cup of coffee at home for between 25 and 50 cents, including the costs of coffee grinds, maker, water, and energy.

The number of cups of coffee imbibed in a single day is 281 million, and the percentage of humans hopped up on caffeine every day is 80. That is a lot of money being made and a lot of productivity being produced.

One wonders how many lives are being saved.

Cosmos

A child asks, "Papa, back years ago the moon was all clean, with no craters?"

The question arrests you. Back when? Before…all of *this*? Will this place be clean again, too? Would that be better or worse than the present state of things, this situation we call "progress"?

Every night you look up at the stars and the moon with your children, and each night the celestial bodies seem to beckon more. Or mock your delicate sense of self-importance. But to the children, they are just lights in the sky—illuminating and magical and intimate.

There are up to 40 billion planets in the universe that are likely habitable. The child reminds you that to other beings in the universe, *we* are the aliens. You remind her that to count to a billion one second at a time would take 31.7 years.

Costumes

"I love you with all my butt," says the four-year-old festooned as a firefighter. He adds, "I would say heart, but my butt is bigger."

Grandma does not mind for a number of reasons, not the least of which is that she's in hospice and can no longer go to the bathroom by herself.

When Grandma was four years old, she was already reading Charles Dickens. This child shall never read Charles Dickens. According to popular lore, Charles Dickens was paid by the word, but historical documentation says he was paid after each 32-page installment. So it was more or less by the word.

This child will be paid by the hour, most likely—if he's lucky. If he's luckier, his work costume will be paid for by his employer.

This grandma will ask what time it is more than on the hour, and want a digital clock put right next to her pillow. When the hospice nurse arrives for the daily check-in, this grandma will tell this child to take off his firefighter suit. Instead of the nurse saying otherwise, he will tell this grandma that the child can't take off the outfit until the fire has been put out.

Of course this nurse is not wearing a costume, not even a nurse's scrubs which are for the hospital, not for home visits. In the car, this nurse will clock his half-hour visit as an hour. Who can blame him? The average 40-hour workweek only accounts for 22.5 hours of actual work anyway, and helping the elderly into their death masks is work outside of time.

Data

A search of *The New York Times* retrieves 310,796 results for articles featuring *data*.

"How 5 Data Dynamos Do Their Jobs" turns out to be a piece about how journalists are increasingly expected to be data analysts; the newspaper now runs workshops to train journalists in gathering and interpreting complex spreadsheets of numbers.

The newspaper also promises more "groundbreaking" data-driven articles to come. But Big Data doesn't give two shits about being groundbreaking; it just sits there dormant until harnessed into meaning, into *facts*. What are the facts?

One is, as the article notes, that "Data is now seamlessly woven into almost everything we do." Does that mean data is objective, subjective, or something else entirely—like the product of handiwork?

The controllers of data are strong leaders who assess vast quantities of numbers in order to execute innumerable decisions at multiple scales. This sounds a lot like capitalism: "Capitalism is now seamlessly woven into almost everything we do."

The proof? The second *Times* result in the search reads "Salesforce Bets on Big Data With $15.3 Billion Tableau Buy," and the third result promises "How Data Can Help You Win in the Winner-Take-All Economy."

Big Data appears to rule the world—and why not? It's a big world!

Tell it to a little kid at the dinner table, though, and soon everything gets upended. Buttery shrimp hits the floor, the five-second rule gets invoked, and then the kid won't touch it, more or less listen to a bullet point you read earlier in the day about "nightmare bacteria." And your capital, real or metaphoric, becomes so much fake money in a toy cash register, later torn or sucked up in the vacuum.

Death

It could happen on the way to work, in the car, after a school bus has barrelled through a yellow light and a child chokes on a spitball but lives to tell the tale (not about you, the dead).

It could be instant, the clap of a thunderbolt, the shudder after fucking, or perhaps more awkward and forgotten, like a room of kindergarteners learning how to snap their fingers for the first time.

The kindergartener asks, "Papa, what does the word *dead* mean?"

"It means what we were before we were alive."

This clarifies nothing.

The younger child asks, "Papa, is dying like melting?"

That sounds about right.

"Like cheese?"

"What?"

"The cheese stick. In my lunch today. I forgot to eat it."

"Yes, honey, it's dead now."

Dentist

Knock on wood.

Diapers

What happened to that perfect kelly green diaper cover? The reusable one that held every drop of piss and shit and never leaked? The one that lasted through two children? The one that could be used from newborn to 24-months? (All those adjustable snaps!) The one that cocooned the washable organic cotton inner-pads perfectly? Where did it go? Do you really want to know? Huggies. Pampers. Eco-friendly and made from bamboo. Rolling hills often disguise landfills.

Dinner

You can cat a 20-ounce bag of potato chips in one sitting with little problem. In rare cases, a bag of potato chips may suffice as dinner. This does not apply to any member of the family under age 14 or over 65. There are rules, after all, at the dinner table even if the dinner table is merely any surface relatively clear of debris.

A child asks, "What does McDonald's serve for dinner?" When you reply, "The dinner menu is the same as their lunch menu," this triggers a sadness unlike one you have ever seen on the boy's face.

Your mother always referred to fast food meals as "a sandwich," as in, during a long road trip, "Do you want to get a sandwich?" It didn't make a difference if it was lunch or dinner.

It is true that Dad was always the one to carve the turkey, expertly handling the electric knife so that no meat was wasted, and that now the task seems herculean especially since you recently read that 204 million pounds of perfectly edible turkey end up in the garbage after each Thanksgiving meal.

That is apparently something like a half pound for every person in the U.S., including infants who can't masticate turkey but discluding undocumented immigrants who can.

Dishes

They want you to play after dinner. But there are the dishes. So many. *How many dishes?* they want to know. They count the dishes. You have 17 left, then 16. Oops, didn't count that fork—back to 17. No matter; this is your time.

Doing dishes can be an ordinary Zen practice, everyone knows that. Or they should. One item at a time—suds, scrub, rinse, set aside. Repeat. Different shape, different dimensions. Nothing ever the same, learn the patterns.

When a child dries dishes alongside you for the first time—wrapping each spoon in a towel, laying it carefully on the countertop—you may find yourself in a fugue state, not ever wanting it to end. The magic of doing a job together. Getting it done. If only this could last. Three. Two. One.

"Now can we go play," they say.

Here, you've been playing all along.

Dreams

"Papa, in my dreams you're a nightmare."

This isn't what dreams were supposed to turn out to be. A soulmate, a child, a house, a car, a cat or two.

Once in three years, everyone in the house wakes up from the same dream, rehashing it over breakfast.

Drinking

And never admit that you enjoy getting inebriated with your kids. Not *with* your kids, exactly, as in they are drunk too, unless you mean *punch drunk*, which, yes, they are…in that playful mode…while you are drunk, very drunk, having the time of your life.

Are they not the best drinking buddies ever?

Do not talk about this outside of the home. Do not put it in writing. Do not become known for performing papa's waltz. No one wants to hear about that. Keep it in the family, as they say. Or just keep it to yourself. Researchers say that people keep approximately nine secrets at a time, five of which they never tell anyone.

Emotions

How to manage my own emotions when I'm trying to manage a child's?

Good question, bad question, or wrong question?

Emotions are a rabbit hole once you start thinking about it. Are they "yours" at all? Why are they so fickle? Do we ever really learn anything about how to control them, or do we just get better at inhabiting the thin shell of selfhood that keeps us intact?

To emote is to dwell in a nebulous realm between feeling and thinking, between reaction and response. You can write emotionally, but it is nearly impossible to write about emotions. Researchers suspect that emojis have seriously fucked up human emotions, but the full data won't be in on that for a decade.

Eight out of ten people deny they are controlled by their emotions. You will run into those eight people, from time to time, the one who will flip you the bird as they pass you on the road, another who will get in your face at the car wash. You think you're not one of those people, until of course you find yourself yelling at your son because he's done exactly the thing you told him not to do: open the car door in traffic.

Empathy

Children's tears depend on a game of tag. But often when you're it, you're also not it.

Fishing

Most of the time you never catch anything. But that is never really the point. Or not the only point. It is something else, about time away or time alone or being in a time that is outside of time.

Then you take them with you and they ask, "Are we going to eat the fish if we catch it?" You try to explain catch-and-release. You say this is why it's called "fishing" and not "catching." But tempers are already in full swing. The canoe is rocking. They want to eat the fish. You keep the next two bluegills you catch, conk them on their heads and throw them in a bucket, take them home, scale them, gut them, and fillet them. You batter them in flour and fry them in butter. They eat them like potato chips, licking their fingers.

That night, all you can imagine is the vacant circular nest where those two fish should be swimming. You are caught in a loop and cannot get out.

Flowers

"I think a bouquet is supposed to have an odd number of flowers because both people are odd."

"I think the person who catches the bouquet is the odd person out."

"I think they are sad, Mom. Look how wilty they are."

"I think the red ones are covered with blood."

"I think the yellow ones are filled with eggs."

"I don't know what to think about the things poking out of the flowers."

"Dad, what are those flowers doing on the counter? The cat is going to knock them over. Be more fucking careful."

You wonder if the f-bomb was learned from you or your wife. You wonder at how the f-bomb is used as though it's no big deal. Your other child wanders the house quietly muttering "Oh fock, oh fock"—sweetness in bloom.

Forests

One third of the world still builds a fire to cook dinner. The smoke from each fire amounts to smoking 30 cartons of cigarettes. Nothing to worry about as the number of forests is decreasing; that is, if forests are still composed of trees.

Some seem to be made up like stories told at night in a child's bed, looking up at the ceiling you assume is there though you can't quite see because it's so dark that your eyes cannot fully adjust.

When you find that first gray hair, it turns out to be white. It turns out to be merely a birch tree in the forest you've been hiking through all your life.

Forts

When all 14 cookbooks are lugged from the kitchen into the family room. When the sheets won't withstand being stretched over the armchair and the piano bench for which you wish you owned a piano. When the pillows of the couch are stood up and turned into walls.

Then you remember the enormous cardboard box that held the neighbor's new refrigerator and in which you made a home with your sister.

Now, she's on the phone, and you're relaying the children's newest construction. It's supposed to be a joyous nostalgia trip—and your sister laughs audibly—but your lasting thought is how many years you wasted not being her friend. When you sit down to calculate the exact number, it seems to be between 12 and 13 years—at least according to Facebook. Someday the parent company Meta shall convert you and your sister to pure consciousness, rejoining you both, fortified forever.

Friends

The children bring home friends. Some of them you get to know and see regularly. Others, it's a one-time deal. Still others phase in and out over the years. Meanwhile, you struggle to keep adult friendships going.

According to a study in the *Journal of Social and Personal Relationships* it takes about "50 hours of time with someone before you consider them a casual friend, 90 hours before you become real friends, and about 200 hours to become close friends." Beyond 200 hours the outcomes are murky, and inversions may occur.

Glitch

The rogue line that appears across your daughter's video game console. You can neither fix it nor console her that it really doesn't matter in the grand scheme of things. When she presses you on what exactly the *grand scheme* of things *is*, your heart skips a beat.

God

Like many parents, you do not find questions about deities irrelevant, you simply find them irritating. Something to explain your way out of with a small person.

"Papa, what's the difference between God and Godzilla?"

"If God made everything, who made Him?"

"Does God have a penis? Well, does He?!?"

"If they call God our father, who is our mother?"

You wonder about the capitalization of the pronoun in the small person's school notebook: Is it still necessary? How much of tradition is best practice and how much is arbitrary rule? How long will you have to stay at Grandma's this year over Christmas break? Will you have to go to Midnight Mass? How come 17% of Americans believe in heaven but not hell?

It all becomes a little much until the three-year-old comes home from daycare belting out *Yes, Jesus loves me...for the Bible tells me so*.... He sings it again and again, and you wonder if your little atheist heart has ever been more touched.

With the last child, you start referring to the universe as *she* to see if it sticks.

Grass

"What is the grass?" asks Walt Whitman's imaginary offspring. It was easier to answer in 1855 when there were no suburban lawns. The average suburban yard contains 4.2 million blades of grass over a lifespan, requiring over 300 gallons of water each year to keep it green.

The New Yorker once reviewed a book that forwarded a theory about exactly why Americans are obsessed with their lawns. The most common kinds of grass are species cultivated to prohibit two things at any cost: sex and death. Lawn grass is cut before it can reproduce, and endlessly watered so it lives on and on and on. At least that's the fantasy.

For a time on the iPad you could download Grass: an app that shows waving blades of grass, which you or your children could fondle on the surface of a smudged screen.

"What is grass?" your third child asks. She tumbles in the green, hurling her little body into the turf.

It makes you think: Does anybody call cannabis *grass* anymore?

The flag of my disposition, Whitman writes in the book he edited and re-edited all the way to his grave. Grass, he writes, *the beautiful uncut hair of graves*. Perhaps he didn't believe in weeds.

Your child spins and falls, makes "grass angels" in the thick blades. You take a picture to savor the moment, text it to your wife.

The following morning the child is covered in itchy red welts. The grass was full of chiggers, who were telling a different story all the while.

Hide-and-Seek

The average U.S. home contains 300,000 items, and 25% of people who have a garage can't park their cars in the garage because there's no room for them. If you eliminate clutter, 40% of your housework goes away. If you walk, ride a bike, or take the bus, you can forgo buying a car and thus have more room in your garage. If you stop leaving your house, you have another problem to contend with.

Armoire comes from the Latin *armorium,* a place where soldiers stored their weapons and armor on long journeys. If you need to get away from your children for a little while, say for a nap, you can climb into the armoire or hide behind all that stuff in the garage. Assemble tent, roll out camping mattress, crawl into sleeping bag. Your wilderness. You're wilderness. If you have a car, you can scrunch into the trunk as the backseat will be occupied by child car seats which are always too much trouble to get in and out. (Make sure there is an air hole, otherwise your partner may be arrested for homicide.)

As you hide, consider what deep fears your children hold about the closet. Can you get lost in this place? Can you get lost in the connotation of the closet, and come out of it with a new identity? Who are you truly? Have you lost something? A life not lived? A loved one? A memory that's now just a bauble in a box?

Get outta there. Don't you remember last year, when the shelving of your daughter's closet collapsed in a jagged heap of smashed faux wood and unworn wool sweaters and junky toys? It is enough to know that she was crouching in the bathtub and not the closet when disaster struck.

Home

The insurance company predicts that you'll live in at least 11 residences in your lifetime. Four of them will be burglarized. Two will sustain storm damage. One will at least partially burn down with or without you in it.

At least one child will fall down at least one staircase. With each second-floor window, the risk of a fatal fall through the screen goes up by 17%. Basements can store power tools, unused bunk beds, Halloween and Christmas decorations, or body parts in bags.

Bob Dylan once famously differentiated between a house and a home. But being there alone in the dark, it doesn't matter what you call it.

Inscrutables

That fork in the dryer. That marble in the rice cooker. That bloody mosquito splattered against an airplane window at 35,000 feet. That corner market down the street advertising BIG SALE but never open. That massive zit on the chin at age 44. That dust bunny the size of a lemon behind the sofa that ends up in the bucket of a toy truck. That Rorschach blot on the wall of the bedroom. That wedding ring temporarily lost in a lover's anus. And now, like some kind of icing on some kind of cake, that neon blue smile painted on the stuffed unicorn. Which one of the whelps has been brushing its teeth with real toothpaste?

Insomnia

After they got all six million skeletons (skulls and femurs) arranged in neat stacks and rows in the Paris catacombs, the architect realized there was a problem: after a while it was all too boring to walk past. Everyone looked the same "de-fleshed." The architect decided to "break up the sinister, grim monotony" by peppering the tunnels with inscriptions from Holy Scripture and from famous poets, artists, and philosophers. You return here in your mind as a strategy for falling back asleep when the witching hour occurs. Sometimes you make it to a line attributed to Nietzsche: "What wilt thou do in the land of the sleepers?"

In the middle of the night, if it's not a child climbing into the bed with you and cuddling close, it's a mantra from Montaigne that won't let you go: "Wake from the sleep of your habits."

Knife

It sits on the kitchen counter too close to the edge. You could touch it...pick it up...but then you might give in to other temptations.

The yellow paring knife has been baiting you for longer than you can recall. You thought you left it up in Michigan, but then your spouse ordered another one because it appeared so pretty in the catalog that came all the way from Kyoto. You face this thing each evening while prepping dinner and again while doing dishes. Then once more the next morning, putting everything away. You can feel the yellow grip in your palm. Your eight-year-old wants to dice carrots with it. You explain it is too sharp for her; she retorts that a sharp knife is less dangerous than a dull one, which she learned from that cooking show she's been binging on Netflix. You don't have a good response to that. You look down at the knife in your hand. The blade is so sharp, and you are so dull. There must be a lesson in this, but you can't figure out what it is.

Laundry

It's a mountain of work, but it's a small mountain as compared to the ocean of liquid laundry detergent your third child just opened up all over the bathroom floor, now as slippery as black ice and nearly impossible to clean up especially after cutting one's middle finger on a shard of a ceramic mug bought years ago at a garage sale and on which is printed *You made it!* in gold letters, indicating that its recipient graduated high school.

A small pink striped sock stuck in a T-shirt, your favorite undies on the lamb in someone else's closet. Even clothes play hide-and-seek.

The mountain can remain for days, a week. Until clean socks and underwear run out, until it overspills the basket and eddies of shirts begin to appear in corners in the hallways. Sometimes you mistake certain soiled articles of clothing—a black and white striped shirt, a pair of rust-colored shorts—for pets you once lived with. It is a soothing notion until you pick the clothes up and there's a memory underneath: the image of yourself trying to dig a pet's grave in the backyard during a torrential rainstorm, your shirt and pants soaked through with water and mud.

Leaf Blower

Wikipedia says the leaf blower was invented by Dom Quinto in the 1950s, but there's no citation and all Google results for Quinto point back to Wikipedia. Wikipedia also says that after the leaf blower was introduced in California, Beverly Hills and Carmel banned it because it was a noise nuisance. *The New York Times* Wirecutter recommends that, after more than 120 hours of research and testing, including "hands-on time with 22 leaf blowers and the input of three pro landscapers with 52 years of combined experience," the best leaf blower is the Worx WG520 Turbine. A 2011 study states that the "pollutants emitted by a leaf blower operated for 30 minutes are comparable to the amount emitted by a Ford F-150 pickup driving from Texas to Alaska." And the University of Rochester's "Calorie Burn Rate Calculator" offers that the estimated calories burned per hour in the act of raking a lawn for an adult of 160 lbs. is approximately 288, which is higher than for dancing a waltz (216) but lower than for operating a snowblower (324). There appears to be no serious research on the experience of children and leaves, whether for raking or jumping into.

Letters

Even though the postal service reports the highest levels of mail on record, people don't hand write as many letters these days, and especially not those from overseas that come in one foldable sheet, blank on one side, and patterned in an envelope shape with red, white, and blue border trim. Lighter than a feather and yet the letter somehow always made it more than 5,000 miles to its addressee. You can still buy stationery for Airmail—the word itself trademarked by the USPS in 2006—strangely, since it's for decorative use only. Airmail as such doesn't exist anymore; it's strictly International Priority or just FedEx.

Regarding letter writing: it rarely happens in an email any longer. When was the last time you sent an email longer than a brief paragraph? When was the last time you included a formal salutation, or a professional signoff? Maybe it was yesterday, and it felt second nature. *Second* nature.

You coerce the kids to write a letter to Grandma. They do it, replete with pictures and birthday wish lists, and you show them how to trifold the letter and place it in an envelope. You find a Forever stamp in the nether regions of a desk drawer. You all walk to the post office and drop the letter in the outgoing mail slot. Somehow none of this is reassuring. Instead, take a piece of paper from the printer tray and sit down and begin that letter you've been meaning to write for years. *Dear Mom and Dad....* It doesn't matter if they're alive or dead. You're not going to mail it anyway. Fold it into a paper airplane, and let the kids see how far it will fly.

Legos

The Apollo landed on the moon in 1969, the same number of blocks in the Saturn V Lego set. The designers loved the symmetry so much that they made it true. And they must especially love space because it is said that the secret of Legos is that every single set—no matter the theme genre or target gender—can be rebuilt into a spaceship.

Your children, however, have decided to stay on Earth. They build an elaborate Lego city in their bedroom. They commandeer an old dining table and several lamps to illuminate the cosmopolis. They spend months saturating the urban simulacra with details and textures. They populate the city with a diverse society of Lego figures, humanoid as well as non-humanoid. In short, they imagine a whole world made out of Lego bricks.

Then one day, they lose interest. The city gradually erodes, parts are cannibalized for other projects, buildings are knocked over by the cat or crushed by the toddler. Eventually they ask for the baseplates to be removed entirely, the stray pieces swept into a bin. The table becomes transformed into something else: a comic club surface, for a different mode of storytelling. They tell you they are no longer "into" Legos.

But you still are. Sometimes walking the kids to school you see random Lego pieces on the ground. It is never certain whether these pieces are intentional trash or have been dropped by accident. This haunts you: somewhere there is a poor child sobbing for just the right missing piece. If only you could show them where it is.

Manners

In the dictionary of manners Cézanne was a pig. So alleged Mary Cassatt after watching him slurp up his dinner in Paris one evening. And so too appear the piggish children, as they riffle through a box of chocolate chip muffins in search of the one with the most chocolate chips. The brown stains on their clothing will only later upset the middle child who, still at age 12, prefers to eat at the counter slouched down so that her shirt catches crumbs from the ledge of her lips like so many survivors leaping into a firefighters' net below. The resulting oily stains from, say, nibbled cheddar cheese or greasy potato chips will not come out even with the latest in stain remover technology inside the shiny-new, metallic pink washer that, along with its stackable dryer companion, costs two months' salary but has a 10-year guarantee, which means that if it lasts such a lifetime, that middle child will be long gone from the house, perhaps finished with college, and doing her own laundry at a laundromat, looking down at one of her shirts, wondering how anyone could ever be so ignoble as to make such a mess. But it is her mother and father who will never fail to come across a crumb on the kitchen floor and think of her and only her.

Math

So that the FDA can approve their anti-aging drugs, some large corporations argue that aging is a disease. No matter. *The Singapore Star* reports that a wiley entrepreneur is developing a so-called "Rip Van Winkle chamber" which will slow down bodily systems by magnitudes so that when you "wake" in the future you will have avoided so much of the mundanity of day-to-day living. The collateral advantage is that you could be closer in age to your children. And if the chambers can slow aging by 40 years, then parents and their children may even be able to spend their dying years together. Or, at least every other generation will be able to benefit from such an advanced juxtaposition. Getting the final moments to sync up will prove to be the biggest challenge. A think tank in Brussels is exploring the corresponding relativistic effects, and claims they have the runway to square the circle.

Meetings

On any given workday 11 million meetings are happening in the U.S., and employees attend on average 62 meetings per month. The average size of a meeting is nine members, and the most frequent meeting start time is 11 a.m.

One researcher advocates making meetings more meaningful by having "no talking" meetings, where members write down their responses to questions and queries and hand them to the chair of the meeting, who then either sums up the replies or points to specific issues. This sounds a lot like something we used to call correspondence by electronic mail, before it became email, before it became a spam-induced nuisance and ignorable.

Many believe that meetings get in the way of productivity. How many is difficult to count, even if many studies have tried. The latest figure is 33.4% of meeting participants believe meetings are unproductive. This is particularly accurate of anything deemed a "family" meeting. In the final analysis this number is still remarkably low, given how little is ever accomplished.

When your eight-year-old calls a family meeting about a missing set of fancy colored pencils, you wear the socks your wife got you that read *This meeting is bullshit*. You weren't brave enough to wear them to the company's strategic planning meeting and point them out to your co-worker while your supervisor yammered on about monetizing user-centric e-services. It is conceivable that you might get fired for such a stunt in the workplace. The sock company is not responsible for any probable or improbable outcomes, even if your co-worker wears the socks and you are the one canned for laughing. But now you and your wife must both stifle laughter about them, as first your daughter then your son tell their sides of the story, as you dutifully record the minutes on your company-owned laptop.

Monarch

The Xerces Society for Invertebrate Conservation recently did the count. There are 28,429 Monarch butterflies left. In 1980, there were 4.5 million.

So when you spotted a Monarch in the yard yesterday, you were both amazed and nervous. The nerves turned to dread when you approached and it didn't move. Another goner.

Inside, you placed it on a sheet of loose leaf paper and then underneath your daughter's toy microscope. Luminous. More beautiful than any stained glass window in any church.

In order to preserve the butterfly, you first are supposed to "relax the specimen" by sealing it in a glass jar with a wet paper towel and a few drops of disinfectant to prevent mold. The jar and towel are no problem, but you don't have Lysol or rubbing alcohol. You read that Nabokov would use vodka in a pinch. Why not?

When the insect pins, insect spreading board, and glass slides (to hold down the wings) arrive from the Home Science Company, the kids don't seem to comprehend they should be excited.

"It's a goner, Dad."

"You don't understand—they will soon be extinct!"

Only when the specimen is pinned and mounted behind glass in a wood case you've made by hand, do you realize that you don't understand. You succeeded in making a trophy out of nature. You have preserved nothing but your vanity.

Monsters

The abominable snowman was the monster that lived in the bedroom closet, and was your kid brother's favorite thing to be afraid of. You never understood the fascination, and once took him to the dictionary and pointed out that "abominable" means "morally repulsive."

He didn't care.

You'd wished he would have feared the Yeti...but now there are the high-end coolers and insulated coffee mugs to deal with.

Is life ever what it sets out to be?

The Himalayan Yeti is most likely the Asiatic bear: *Ursus thibetanus*. At least according to people who've done the hard investigating.

And what about Bigfoot, which sounds so much more colloquial, if just as mysterious.

The mean age when a child stops believing in the man who lives at the North Pole is five years and three months. At that moment the tundra ceases to excite. Until the emperor penguins arrive! After they mate, the mother penguin lays an egg, on which the father penguin will sit for 65 days through sub-zero snowstorms while the mother goes off in search of food. A mind of winter is nothing if not very cute. The Sixth Great Extinction is another abomination altogether.

Movies

The first 42 movies you watch with them you'll remember every line, each song. These characters and scenes will stay with you at night, waking you up when the children don't. These movies will nestle somewhere sweet near your heart cavity.

Then the time will come when you stop watching movies with them, but only hear films in the background as you do dishes or sweep or drive. You'll catch snippets of dialogue or grand orchestral scores, but have no idea about the plot points or the story. These movies will exist in the widening chasm between you and your offspring. Do not lament. If not the movies, then their soundtracks can still bring you joy. Dig out the soundtrack to *Frozen* on CD. For a colleague's depth-charging of your pet project, there is no greater tincture than rolling down all the windows of the car on an icy cold winter's morning in order to blast on full-volume *Let it go, let it go…Let the storm rage on… the cold never bothered me anyway…*.

Name Calling

If you do, in the heat of the moment, bark out some kind of epithet like *teenie bitch* or *little bastard*, you'll never live it down: weeks or perhaps months later your son will remind you—because you'll have forgotten it entirely—of that one time you called him a *dickwad* for teasing his sister for the umpteenth time. It doesn't matter if he deserved it or if you said it under your breath or if it occurred after the stress of a very long day.

All days become very long days with children. And all children have better memories than you do, if only because time has yet to teach them what is best forgotten. But maybe you'll have the last laugh. Medical scientists say that the internet generation is already experiencing digital dementia due to excessive screen time: "We predict that from 2060 to 2100, the rates of Alzheimer's disease and related dementias (ADRD) will increase significantly, far above the Centers for Disease Control (CDC) projected estimates of a two-fold increase, to upwards of a four-to-six-fold increase."

In light of what they unleashed upon our children, some technologists responsible for today's addictive gadgetry have called themselves *mad scientists*. Nevertheless, *computer science* as a college major continues to be on the rise.

Napping

Science says that we are 31% more effective in our work when we're in a good mood. But a good mood can be so difficult to sustain. Sometimes one just wants to be in a bad mood, or simply be moody.

Napping can help one's mood, people say.

People say *Nap when they nap*. But people don't say *Poop when they poop*. People should. Because solo pooping is almost impossible. A voice or knock is nearly always at the door. *Can I come in?* If you answer *I'm busy in here* or even *I'm taking a dump*, you will have to answer more simple yet ineffable questions.

Naptime is a no-time, not time to do other things, but once when you were a toddler you were found standing in your crib painting the wall with your own feces, when you were supposed to be napping.

New Year

It's not easy to find data about how successful people are at changing their habits, except for around the new year. Research from the University of Scranton suggests that only 8% of people who set resolutions actually make the changes they intend to. Keep in mind that's 8% of the people who are motivated enough to set resolutions in the first place...which is less than the mere 42% who set resolutions at all.

So let's say you learn about a new food, or a bunch of foods that you believe will truly make a difference—to your health in the long term and to your energy and waistline in the short term. You're motivated enough to make a change...let's say you're as excited as someone in that motivated minority who sets resolutions on New Year's Day. The good news: Congratulations, you're pretty motivated to make a change to your diet! The bad news: You've still got a 92% chance of failing to actually do it.

This statistic does not diminish the exuberance of playing Uno on New Year's Eve, watching as the children get the hang of it and begin to cream you, hand after hand.

Open the champagne, pour the apple juice.

News

They say no news is good news, but this saying falls flat when your toddler goes silent. They are either sabotaging something fragile in the house or pooping on the floor. Or trying to accidentally on purpose smother the kitten with a knitted pot holder. If it is bad enough, it may even make tomorrow's news.

Nighttime

"Daddy, don't go," she says.

Then she embraces you tightly and kisses you hard on the lips as if you're her lover at a train station in a black and white movie. But whenever you see a black and white movie, your first thought is always *These people are all dead*. This now includes you and your daughter.

Noise

"What was that?!?" The sound of someone breaking in, or just the children at play, toppling over a chair or one another? Ninety-eight percent of the time it is the latter (the collective latter). The clangs and thuds of impact may never exceed the allowed decibel level ordinance of the neighborhood, but in your home the noise will always disrupt whatever task or thought you were engaged in, and cause a momentary existential tremor. The expression of when an alarming event "takes a year off your life" is only a poor extrapolation of the nanoseconds of unexpected noises caused by children that chip away at your mortal time on earth. Each crash, scream, and cough that in sum will sonically as well as physically bury you.

Nursing Home

"Do we have to go in there again?" says the four-year-old.

You nod, and push open the broken automatic door.

There she is—your 72-year-old mother—trying to wheel down the hall with one arm. It'll be five months of this until she is gone. You won't tell people she "passed" like a gallstone. You'll say *She's dead, goddammit.*

On the way out, the child is attracted to the little plant in the lobby. She attempts to pick off a leaf. You want to scold her. Instead, you tell her it's a bonsai, a tree which is supposed to live for hundreds of years.

Obstacle Course

Hurdle the trench, climb up the boulder, swing across the creek, dive into the pool.

Wade through the bushes, commando crawl over the grass, sniff the dog poop on your shoe.

Roll out of bed, stumble downstairs, brew the coffee.

Hug the old lady next door, trip over the gardening hose without breaking your neck, refill the little free library with unread classics.

Pajamas

It is ill-advised to show up for work in pajamas. Sleeping in pajamas works for some, others not as well. Some will sleep in pajamas their whole life, others will leave them behind in adolescence. Once the Gymboree shark shorts pajamas are outgrown, there will be no finding a new pair in a bigger size, even used on eBay. Pajamas can be cute or sexy but shall not be both at once, though the line of separation is hazy. No matter the style, it's illegal to fish in pajamas in Chicago.

Pets

He says there's ear hair coming out of her belly button. You explain that a cat doesn't have a belly button.

Is that even true?

The youngest child fears the cat, but the oldest likes to cradle the cat in his arms every chance he gets.

When it comes time for the cat to be put down, you don't use the euphemism because you know they're going to ask *Put her down where?* And you don't tell them she's going to cat heaven because you wouldn't be able to say it with a straight face. You simply tell them to say goodbye to your beloved cat on the morning you've scheduled the visit to the vet. Then when they are off to school, you stand there in the kitchen with the cat in your arms unable to move, tears streaming down your face. A cliché that, for once, you can believe in.

Phones

Your three-year-old collects phones (of which she includes a Casio calculator). There are the old Panasonic cordless landline phones, the walkie-talkies made to look like iPhones, the VTech Baby Swipe & Touch phone, an old Pantech, and even an old TV remote control that is, to her, a phone.

When your new smartphone falls and its screen shatters, you revert to an older model that had been relegated to the back of a drawer. It is considerably smaller, antiquated by a few years. Your drunk seatmates on a flight to Denver heckle you for its diminutive size and outdated style. They take pictures of you holding it up. The looks on their faces say *Dumb fuck*.

Back home you threaten to go further back, to your old Nokia bar phone. The kids threaten back that they will refuse to be seen with you if you do. You buy a pared-down Light Phone instead: no internet, black and white, just phone and text messages. It still looks sleek, and so this manages to assuage your children and accomplish a decisive downgrade. You write this story on the new phone, haltingly, getting accustomed to its different dimensions and feel. It is slow going yet that is the point now, isn't it? Don't worry, regardless of the phone you have, in a few years your children won't want to be seen with you anyway.

Plastic

Whales cannot pass plastic, which accumulates into a nearly calcified form in their bodies. A beached whale was found in the Philippines with 88 pounds of plastic in its gut. It died of plastoxicity. Inside the stomach, there were various single-use plastic bags and heaps of shards or pieces of plastic less than five millimeters in length: microplastics.

Phytoplankton especially feast on such microplastics, which is either odd or perfectly reasonable since plastics are made from fossil fuels (not to be mistaken for fossils) that are, partly, composed of phytoplankton which are 419.2 million to 358.9 million years old.

By examining human excrement, researchers have determined that we are ingesting microplastics and pooping them out. How much we are keeping in our bodies—intestines and particularly the liver—is not yet known. "We've mismanaged our waste," says a researcher at the University of Toronto, "and it's come back to haunt us at our dinner table. We are literally eating our own trash."

Poop

In our language's lexicon, we have so many words for it depending on the connotation one is after: excrement, dung, dogpile, rabbit turd, crap, dump, shit, and of course poop. Having small children, you will be amazed how much you think and talk about something you preferred to not think and talk about before. In a human's infancy, poop begins as a pleasant yellow, more mush than kernel. The smell is strong but sweet, and it washes off easier than most things save the homemade boysenberry jam a neighbor left on your doorstep.

Keep this in your head, or your muscles, as the poop evolves over time. Mark the days by poops planned for, successfully shat, cleaned up, and anticipated again. Eventually your own poop will increasingly fascinate or preoccupy. It will have to—because someday when you stop pooping, you will begin what is called "actively dying."

Porn

In early adolescence a clothing catalog used to suffice for porn, even if you didn't use the word for it. You hadn't yet learned the expressions "rub one off" or "shoot your load."

Now on a business trip to Tokyo, instead of a Bible in the drawer of the dresser in the hotel there is a pamphlet for the Peach Channel on adult TV. Each of the nipples of the women is covered by a pink peach in the shape of an upside-down ♡.

When the children start writing self-proclaimed "X-rated" comics, the parents are best advised to stand down. To take a load off. To wait and see. A watched pot never boils.

Privacy

Alone at last in the shower at midnight.... Until you detect a squeaking noise that is neither old pipes nor a mewling cat. Baby at arms? Baby in arms. Baby in arms in the rocker. Rocker. Rocker. Rock her.

How many licks does it take before one can't stand it any longer and is forced to bite the lollipop? What happens when there's no chewy chocolate center you used to love or that once loved you? What happens when the lollipop is a nipple?

The delirium that accompanies a fussy baby in the middle of the night. It's private, sure. To be alone with her in your arms. Then the phone buzzes on the nightstand. It's the credit card company or a newsfeed or worse an emoji from an old friend. She must be bored in the privacy of the nursery, too. What is commiseration but a slug of whiskey from a tumbler which no algorithm can predict—over distance and between friends.

Quiet

You can't ever experience complete silence. And if you could, wouldn't that terrify the absolute hell out of you?

The answer is a measured *yes*. There exist super silent rooms, called anechoic chambers, in various labs around the world. At Orfield Laboratories in Minnesota, for example, no one has ever lasted for more than 45 minutes in such outer-space quietude. The oddest thing, perhaps, about these chambers are the hundreds of wave- and radiation-absorbing spikes that line the walls, ceiling, and floor—all their points pointed right at you.

Silence is not the same thing as quiet. Quiet is what you want your whelps to be most of the time. But when it's too quiet in the back bedroom, something is probably wrong. And when you're getting the silent treatment from the other adult in the room, it is unmistakably loud.

A word of advice: Should you be traveling south on I-65 through Nashville, just south of the city is a Hyatt Place Hotel that doubles as a sleep study center for a local university. The hotel is exceptionally quiet—ample signage insists on this—and should you be nursing heartache or an otherwise melancholic soul, the hotel can soothe with its absence of sounds. All the usual raucous bumps, bangs, and shrieks of other accommodations are absent here, all in service of the science of sleep.

Rainbow

A child asks to paint a rainbow and demands a demonstration. You dutifully paint seven arcs, ROYGBIV. The child takes her turn, choosing only black paint: seven opaque arcs. And looks up, proud of her rainbow.

That you can only view a rainbow with your back to the sun is merely true. Just as there are seven colors in a rainbow, six strings on a guitar, five fingers in a fist, four horsemen of the apocalypse, three little words, two kinds of people, and one day when it'll all make sense.

Regarding zero, there is no approximation.

Reality

We live in a reality mediated by screens. If we question the use of screens, it's as a means of getting attention, a means of showing off what we think we know about a world without screens. Cf., *Limit your screen-time!*

Children potentially offer the world's greatest resistance to the reign of screens. But not because they are less prone to be on screens. They may be addicted to screens, but they will still resist our ideas of order: *Stop throwing the ball in the house! All those crumbs, can't you eat a little neater? Get going, we're running late! Don't forget your iPad!*

Screens or no screens, their reality is different from ours, and will win out in the end.

As for adults who don't have children, they still carry their own childhoods with them, whether they like this reality or not.

Refrigerator

To keep bacteria at a minimum, the fridge should be kept at 37 degrees and the freezer at 0. That takes a family only so far, meaning if a toddler keeps leaving the knee-level freezer ajar so that Mom or Dad wakes up to find thawed chicken thighs and soupy ice cream pints and something that looks like it might have been brown bananas saved for smoothies all congealed into a sweating mess, then it's simply one more piece of work that love requires.

After a hurricane-caused power outage, it seems that your evaporator fan is kaputt, prohibiting your fridge from cooling lower than 50 degrees but allowing your freezer to cool to the point that the interior resembles a subarctic diorama, one perfect for the kids' Star Wars snowtroopers. With the help of a General Electric technician, you discover that the evaporator fan is perfectly fine. But the fridge requires some kind of software update after the power outage, one that is incompatible with the existing evaporator fan. Thus, the technician unpackages and installs a new one. As he leaves, he hands you the four-year-old evaporator fan, which looks impressive, even still new, its four black matte plastic blades unblemished. You fantasize about rigging it up to a battery, getting it spinning again just for the hell of it. For months, it will lie in your kitchen junk drawer, a reminder of sweltering heat, a cipher of cool.

Restaurant

One out of every two children goes ballistic in a restaurant. These odds may sound favorable, but when not ballistic, the other options fragment into five remaining paths: happy, docile, dejected, ornery, and resigned. To the point: the odds are not in your favor to have a happy child dine with you at a restaurant. On the other hand, 73% of adults at restaurants are secretly seething. In the final analysis when it comes to eating out, children turn out to be just downsized adults who are perhaps only slightly more expressive. They may even enjoy their food.

Romantics

William Wordsworth once said "the child is the father of the man."

William Blake thought childlike innocence was on a short and slippery continuum with the guiltiest pleasures and most horrific atrocities.

Emily Dickinson referred to her poems as "disobedient children" and "youthful debauches."

A fringe theory holds that Samuel Taylor Coleridge's ancient mariner is an anachronistic homage to Greta Thunberg.

John Keats was apparently not a bookish child.

When it came to children, Lord Bryon [redacted].

Henry David Thoreau supposedly cuffed a schoolchild once, but the little bastard probably deserved it.

Mary Shelley dispatches Victor Frankenstein's kid brother with shocking efficiency.

Ralph Waldo Emerson had a lot to say about the American scholar, but experts cannot agree on the ideal age that Emerson had in mind for this nascent genius.

Charlotte Smith understood that we're all just kids and that the teacher has left the building.

"Give me a child until he is seven years old," said St. Ignatius Loyola, "and I will show you the man." Only God knows what Iggy meant; he was no Romantic.

Salami

You almost lost it when the lunch kits started getting brought back home from school, unopened. Still sealed in their packages but no longer safe for re-refrigeration, much less consumption.

The crackers were easy enough to deal with: they could be pulverized into fine dust and repurposed to feed the red-headed finches in the backyard. The cheese squares were slightly more complicated, but a Google search turned up a method for melting the cheese down, whereupon it could be used for tortilla chip dip.

It was the salami rounds that stymied you. What does one do with so much processed pork? It was always the promise of bite-sized protein that made the kits more than a snack, indeed into a government-approved meal despite the "hog holocaust" happening in the Midwest.

Ultimately, you fed the salami to your neighbor's dog, whose best friend you were for a number of weeks. His untimely death two months later may or may not correlate with the overfeeding of the salami.

Sandwich

A sandwich can be two pieces of bread with a slice of bologna or cheese in the middle. Or both. A sandwich can even be just the two slices of bread, taken apart and munched one slice at a time, or torn into pieces and thrown to seagulls.

Kids sometimes feel sandwiched between their parents, or one another. Have you ever made a sandwich out of pillows, with a child as the "meat"? Have you ever played hide the salami?

In spring 2019, the sandwich industry was disrupted by replacing traditional bread buns with a giant pickle, sliced in half.

"Oh hell," says your partner, "when you think about it, everything is a sandwich. Armpits, buttocks. Sofa cushions."

"Yes," you say, "the world squeezes us between firmament and soil."

Screens

Studies show that prolonged exposure to screens has been correlated with exponential surges in myopia among people under 18. What this means for the future of the species is inconclusive, but various hypotheses suggest that by 2042 the human figure could be shaped in a way nearly unrecognizable to today's standards of beauty and normative body types. While the neck will crane over and arguably attain new levels of curvature (and perhaps seductive force), arms and legs will almost certainly atrophy, and worse, the human buttock will bloom into what in anatomical terms can only best be called a "pad." This biomorphic shift will be a necessary sacrifice or really an evolutionary movement in service of the screens that are sure to command more attention as cryptocurrency overcomes traditional economic models and as being together, as in, *you and me*, is re-rendered as a remote encounter, as efficient as it is vivid on the glowing surface toward which our eyeballs gravitate, and increasingly, stick.

See also *Authority*, *Self-actualization*, and *Porn*.

Security

A recent survey conducted by the Syracuse Holistic Initiative Team found that people feel the most secure when in their beds. Vulnerability is also reported at its peak when people are in bed beneath the covers, especially when naked. That popular pillowcase was never about its actual fabric or feel. The concept of a "security blanket" means more than an infantile neurosis or a mere developmental tool.

When you finally secure the down payment and purchase your first home, it may come equipped with an elaborate security system that depends on every single window and door being shut tight. When attempting to arm the alarm for the first time, shortly after putting the children to bed, the siren may suddenly sound, awakening everyone and causing no small sense of panic and insecurity. Following several minutes of suspense and a frantic hunt around the house armed with your childhood hatchet (blade still sharp), the culprit may be discovered: an outdoor storage closet, where shoes are kept, has been cracked open by a zephyr. Tucked back in bed and the security system safely disarmed, slide the hatchet behind the headboard. It's perfectly okay now to dream of lone wolves and dark forests.

Self-Actualization

The oldest child calls you "annoying and weird," the middle child scratches your face, and the youngest pitches what seems to be a fit over not being able to drink Mommy and Daddy's wine from the bottle.

When the middle child begins a sentence with "Who was the first person ever to—," you instinctively yelp *me, myself, and I.*

Because you don't know who else to be, *Be your own self* seems like either an abstruse idea or one always just out of reach. With children, this problem is redoubled: they can't simply be themselves any more than you can just be you.

Now, do you remember who you once wanted to be?

Sex

In some countries, people shag air-filled, life-sized dolls.

In others, they pork pillows made of the finest down.

In Sweden, a news program called *Kalla Fakta* (Cold Facts) ran an exposé: apparently "live-plucking" fowl is a thing—in China and Poland.

In Hungary, it's estimated that "40 to 45 percent of feathers have been live-plucked by experienced 'rippers' who are paid piece-rate." Live-plucked ducks yield softer feathers?

What the fuck.

If you are happy, you want to kiss. Or you kiss in an effort to bring about a certain happiness. Sometimes the effort and the desire amount to the same thing: no sex.

Why bother spelling s-e-x in front of the children after they've learned to spell—or after that time the four-year-old walked in on you two humping in bed but with your shirts still on. You should not have pushed it: 23 minutes is the optimum amount of time to spend toward climax for both parties. Or so says a friend of a friend.

According to *Bustle*, a site aimed at millennial women, achieving an orgasm with your partner at the same time isn't necessarily something to strive for. "It's OK if one of you reaches it first, then the other reaches theirs within a minute or so. This is still considered reaching an orgasm together."

On the timeline of the existence of the universe, starting at 0 and ending at 24 hours, humans have been around for less than a minute.

Shots

A pandemic happens and the kids are excited to get their shots. At the doctor's office, they flex their muscles and mug from behind their masks. They wear their *I got the shot!* stickers proudly.

Amid all the hand-wringing, obfuscating, and haranguing about public health and the proper response to an outbreak, the children are a model of civility. Watch and learn.

Slugs

On the first morning of school, a child doesn't want to get out of bed. You snuggle with him and ask what's wrong.

"You know how people say they have butterflies in their tummies? I have slugs in my tummy."

You know that feeling. You still have that feeling most days. You try to empathize and reassure the child, but sharing the anxiety further contaminates the morning.

Then you remember the slime—the sticky stuff his sister loves more than any toy. You take out the dishwashing soap and school glue and make up a batch. Your son constructs the snails out of Legos, and you make the slimy slug's trail. It is a simple pleasure. You tell him this and are slightly stunned when he replies, "Is there any other kind?"

Snowflakes

The connotation of their supposed individual uniqueness has become less and less important. It's their ability to fall suddenly and accumulate that worries you and others on the road. Car accidents are the number one cause of death for people under the age of 34. In snowy climes, the probability skyrockets. Your best hope may be traveling alone. (Polar ice caps melting does not mean snowflakes will stop falling anytime soon, though they may no longer be as white as snow.)

Space

The child pulls on your sleeve: "Mama, did you know the earth is just a little rock in space?"

"Yesterday you said the earth was just a crumb to the universe," the older child interrupts. "Get your story straight."

The younger child doesn't understand what a "straight" story is.

Everything is suddenly inexplicable.

Spill

Neither a sin nor a crime. Not even a big deal. You might try telling the child that pouring milk into a cup is simply "spilling with intent."

The child will proceed to pour the cup of milk on the floor—a different kind of intent.

Stairs

A child reflects: "You know what would be really bad? If someone fell down a hundred stairs. And they were cement."

Fact is, stairway accidents are the second leading cause of accidental injury, after car accidents. Fact is, 12,000 people die each year at the bottom of the stairs.

The average two-story house has a staircase with 13 steps, and stair-climbing is a great way to get a cardiovascular workout— for free! And brain development occurs exponentially when children learn to climb stairs. Stair gates are a necessary modern safety precaution, but they have arguably impaired the evolution of the human species.

For every single step that humans climb, they go down at least twice as many.

Stars

One in three children will suffer from irregular sleep patterns. Colic, night terrors, Freudian fidgets, self-induced quasi-suffocation beneath blankets and twisted sheets.

One child, awake well after midnight and soothed by his exhausted father, will look out into the clear northern sky and ask, "Papa, what's all that white stuff behind the stars?"

"That? That's the Milky Way. It's more stars."

The son will say "woah" and finally fall into a fitful slumber. While astronomers have counted 170 billion galaxies at the time of this writing, there never appear to be enough celestial bodies to quiet the human mind.

Success

When your 16-year-old comes back from their first job interview, they tell you all about the platform they will be working on. The company acquired lots of material recently, and it is your child's job to accelerate it to the next level. They have to file weekly progress reports, but they are open-ended. And all of the product is technically free; no one owns anything. They think of it as a co-op of the mind. This is their success model. There are three phases to tackle. Phase one is development of a new platform. Phase two is data input and phased roll-out. Phase three is implementation at scale. The first phase will require 300 hours, roughly ten hours a week plus a few sprints, completion by February. That accounts for the holidays ahead too. The company is super flexible. The deadline seems doable. Your child admitted to the company that they were recently diagnosed with ADHD, but they were assured this wouldn't be a problem. Apparently studies have shown that profit margins widen according to the number of employees with documented cases of attention deficit hyperactivity disorder. They all have it. It's what has made the company so successful.

Swimming

If you wear the pink polka dot bikini, it'll rankle the other moms who wear the one-piece suits with strategically placed frills and skirts to hide sagging parts. Or they don frocks people used to call "butt shields." It's true that it was nice to have breasts that held up on their own. But if one more mom mommysplains about the need to give your toddler swim lessons, you may have to strangle her with her own thong.

Tantrums

Yesterday, you screamed the phrase *You goddamn ungrateful little shits!* Today, you're merely obdurate, a word you imagine they will correctly identify on a vocabulary test someday in high school. And think fondly back on you.

For the new year you make a resolution: *No more yelling at the kids.* Even when the pre-pre-teen screams at you, you are equanimous. As his mouth moves, you focus on the inside of it. There's still a gap where a canine dropped out last week. The tooth fairy gave him five dollars. His sister was mad when he told her the tooth fairy isn't real. She turned to you: "Liar!"

But you never told her about the tooth fairy. She's not upset because you lied, but because the tooth fairy never existed in the first place. This seems to be the problem with reality: it's both too much and never enough.

Teasing

Teasing begins most often between two children, and ends almost always in an argument between two adults.

Time Change

For those with children, the semiannual spring forward/fall back is the bane of existence. Well-rehearsed schedules and logistics get cocked up and thus do children's clocks. There are meltdowns and misery. It takes weeks to right the ship.

Perennially, a movement crests to eliminate daylight savings, replete with congressional motions and votes in the offing. This whole charade of time change (or the charade of its dispatch) may soon be but a memory of fumbling and foibles.

But is the charade really all that miserable? Is the bane really the "agent of death" that Middle English says it is?

More importantly, what if we miss the time change? What if there were things in these biannual rituals that, against all odds, maintained our cohesion, nay our very sanity? Whatever comes of this proposed revision, there will be no going back—in either direction.

Toilet Seat

For reasons unknown the six-year-old likes taking photos of the toilet. Particularly in the dark. An interest in black holes? This while one's partner is googling why the 12-year-old has such wild mood swings and whether it's a sign of a serious psychiatric disorder. It's 7:22 a.m., and one must head to the other toilet for a few minutes of peace and quiet and a good shit. As soon as the ass hits the seat, there's an issue. The seat is loose again. Stripped nuts below? Cracked plastic screw? The slow-close toilet seat did seem cheap at the home improvement store, but they all seemed cheap. Cheep? There's that sound again: the six-year-old making his morning bird coos. It is not unpleasant.

Trains

Almost everyone who still rides a train in the United States is poor, old, or European. The poor believe trains are cheaper than flying; the old are too terrified of flying; and, the Europeans prefer trains because they're accustomed to the miles of efficient, state-run tracks in their home countries.

None of this is information to emphasize while playing with toy trains or touring a steam engine. For that matter, perhaps nothing at all is important to emphasize while playing with or in trains. Or playing with or in anything. In fact, information is largely irrelevant to much of playing with a child. The point is in the playing, and in seeing yourself as a thing at play. Your child's favorite plaything, in other words, is you, Passenger.

Trash

When you bought the cute trash cans for each child's room, you made sure to select sizes, colors, and themes that matched their personalities. A month later, the trash cans were filthy buckets of chewed gum, gobs of tape, assorted wrappers, pencil shavings, used tissues, and chunks and crumbs of no longer discernible foodstuffs. No matter how fast you empty them, they are brimming again the next time you check. While what the children throw out does reveal new aspects of their personalities, you do wonder what will happen down the road. After the children leave home, that is, how does one precisely throw out a trash can?

Treasure

What you find between couch cushions, the mysteries of the vacuum chamber, the plastic shard on the floor, the glitter or cat litter deep in the bedsheets, the amputated Star Wars action figure's hand in the pocket of a winter coat, pennies in dark corners, panties in your shirt sleeve, rusty nails in dirt, a flower from a weed, a Barbie's turquoise high heel behind the bookshelf, dried mandarin peels in the footwells of the car, a crayon drawing of your family crumpled on top of the refrigerator. Each day a treasure, but never a sunken ship. Or is that what the house really is?

They say three million ships are at the bottom of the world's oceans, and less than one percent of them have been explored. Of the remaining 99%, it is estimated that half contain something of value. Unless you're a lionfish, in which case the wreck *is* the treasure.

Vasectomy

Standing in line at the pharmacy, a dozen people behind you. The pharmacist has lost your prescription and riffles through a mound of papers. "I have two orders for valium—for one tablet, or 60. Which is yours?" With everyone staring, you admit that yours is for one tablet. You feel scowls rake your back.

You take the valium tablet as you sign in to the clinic, chewing it up as the doctor suggested. You feel no great release or euphoria. The numbing needle burns as it is injected into your testicles, first right, then left. You feel the deep pulls of the vas as the doctor slices and cauterizes. You smell your own singed biomatter.

Later, at home recovering, the valium finally kicks in. When you get up to pee for the first time, you faint and crack your nose and forehead on the back of the toilet. Your wife catches you as you collapse onto the cold tile floor, unconscious. A child, having heard the fall and the cry of your wife, wanders in to see if everything is okay. All of this is recounted to you later, after you regain consciousness. Everyone's a little scared and jittery. No more solo walks to the bathroom; you are given a bedpan to pee into. You watch *Solo*, alone and without irony.

It may be the residual effects of the valium or the general relief of the procedure being over. But still, in those moments of unconsciousness, you are struck by child-like giddiness and a profound realization. Once you fainted there was nothing inside of it, no panic or terror. Just a depthless absence of being, a great calming abyss.

Vegetables

Slice the carrots exactly as requested. Expect 38% to go uneaten.

Celery is good for keeping teeth clean and for fiber. With almond butter and raisins, it becomes an ecological story.

Halved radishes with a smear of butter and pinch of salt are good, but only when fresh.

Call them "veggies" if you must, but for a child they are bargaining chips: "If I eat my broccoli, can I have a chocolate pudding?"

Is this a free market? Is she trading up or down? What is the smartest investment? What is a bond, really?

What connects us to the land and the land to us? Plant a seed and bring it to fruit.

War

You want to shield them from the new horrors that appear daily, hourly. But somehow they find out about them. They talk about the Ukrainians, the Russians, and Putin. They talk about sanctions. They know what a salvo is, which you look up to make sure you know the definition accurately. They keep bringing up Germany, which confuses you. At playdates, one of their 10-year-old friends spits out knowledge about rockets, tanks, minelayers, and whatever else is being used: Gimmlers, M31s, M142 HIMARSs, BM-30 Smerchs, FV104 Samaritans, COBRAs, AGM-114 Hellfires, OTR-21 Tochkas, Switchblade drones, MIM-23 Hawks, Ground Master 200s, UR-77 Meteorits. This tech jargon is not such a problem until the same kid recounts what kind of weapon killed the mother and her nine-year-old and 18-year-old who were trying to cross a bridge to safety outside of Kyiv. You know this story—there was a front-page *New York Times* article about the family—and the photograph of the victims cut up by shrapnel is impossible to erase from your mental storehouse, especially at 3:41 a.m. when you are shocked awake for no ostensible reason other than your monkey mind swinging from catastrophic limb to catastrophic limb.

Although there is no protecting the children from the onslaught of information, you have protected them from the actual war—at least so far. This by virtue of living far, far away from the "bad guys." Or rather by virtue of the fact that your maternal great-grandmother emigrated from Latvia to England (you can't recall her last name now), and your paternal grandfather emigrated from Slovenia to Chicago sometime right before or after World War I. Their individual stories are lost in the annals of history. It occurs to you: Does not knowing them protect you, and if so, from what exactly?

Weekend

There are always too many ideas. Too much to do in one morning, one afternoon. *We can create an airplane out of the recycling! We can put my solar-powered propellor on it to make it go! Let's bake a loaf of pumpkin bread for Mama! No! Let's go fishing in Bayou St. John and catch a real fish we can really eat! Oh, we could build a huge Lego airport with all our airplanes around it and ALL the minifigures going to the airport! What if we draw mazes? Let's make a fort! One that you can fit in! And then we can watch* Spirited Away *in the fort! Can I have something to eat first? But no—first I have to go pee.* Then comes the negotiating and anxiety, topped with the disappointment of an act half accomplished. The recognition of being a shitty parent. *This has been the worstest day ever!* The only control you might exert is in correcting their grammar. But it's not a school day.

Wipes

For the face, hands, and bottom. In that order only, please.

Wisdom

As in business acumen. Not albumen, the clear-to-white stuff of an egg, the stuff the children seem unable to separate from the yolk when making the meringue. *Achoo*, they do well. Snot into the pancake mix, the cookie dough, the cup of your hand. When you wipe it under your armpit, they notice. They will sneeze next time right into your sleeve.

How many times will you chastise your child for picking their nose, only to turn away and pick your own?

Four times, the latest survey concludes. People pick their noses four times a day on average.

Eating the pickings is a different matter: most cultures try to get children to refrain from the practice. Some scientists, though, argue that mucophagy (ingesting nasal mucous) should be promoted: "With the finger you can get to places you just can't reach with a handkerchief. The nose is a filter in which a great deal of bacteria are collected, and when this mixture arrives in the intestines, it works just like medicine."

Wish List

Over the course of 11 years, 167 items populate the family's Amazon wish list. You delete all of them with one click. It's the wish you'd longed for without realizing it was a wish at all—to be free of wanting yet another thing you haven't made yourself.

Wrinkles

The expensive goo is out of the jar.

"Does that stuff really work?"

"Yes."

"Can I have some?"

"It's too late for you."

She's right; the mirror tells the story. The deepest ones are around the eyes. Lines in all directions. Riverbeds? Deltas? No. Asterisks. It'd be too easy to say you've seen too much: the birth of multiple children, the death of multiple parents.

It's not the deaths, it's the dying, stupid.

She's still looking at you in the mirror. It's almost like old times when you both stood half-clothed in a steamy bathroom. There's a slight smile on her face.

No need to point out the slow-growing age spot on her left temple; she knows it's there.

Yoga

The unsourced in-flight magazine article says, "People who practice yoga are 20% more likely to have a positive self-image than those who don't."

In class, the instructor emphasizes to avoid comparing your practice to that of others in the room. It's not a competition; you get that.

At home, however, the child likes to do yoga with you and she does it so much better. Soon you're envious of a three-year-old's downward dog, extended puppy, and half pigeon.

When she asks what Shavasana is, don't hesitate to tell her corpse pose. When she asks what that is, it's fine to say *Just play dead.*

You can do that as well as anyone else.

YouTube

Without the how-to videos, you would be utterly lost in performing home maintenance and improvement tasks, such as fixing the leaky bathroom sink faucet or installing a ceiling fan. Once, you even replaced the drain motor on the 16-year-old dishwasher—thanks to someone who for some reason made a detailed video about it. (It did not seem like someone you would hang out with, in real life.)

Of course, the kids are a different matter. There are no how-to videos on YouTube that help, unless that means for distraction. In fact, all kinds of other videos—from innocuous cartoons to malicious ones ("Peppa Pig Offs Her Papa")—suck up so much of the little ones' hours. This isn't always an ethical issue; it's an economic one. You introduce the phrase "opportunity cost" to the 14-year-old. He understands the concept—as well as "supply and demand"—but shrugs and returns to watching a video of a man winning a contest by eating 72 hotdogs in 10 minutes.

"Dad," he later says, "have you heard about the One Chip Challenge?"

He informs you that there's some kind of meme going around about eating the world's hottest chip—potato, tortilla?—laced with the world's hottest pepper. The Carolina Reaper, which tops two million on the Scoville Heat Units Scale.

"Huh?"

"A jalapeño is about 5,000."

You can kind of get the fascination, but you worry about the fascination. Especially after reading that 40% of teenagers believe their favorite YouTuber understands them more than their real-life friends.

You're not even technically his friend. Where does this leave you in the rankings?

Zero

The concept originated somewhere in India. Circle nothing, someone once said, and there you are. The derivation of the universe.

Now, zero is merely half of binary code.

Or what you feel like each time you take a business trip, even for two days.

When you get back home from that trip, the youngest one may ask at tuck-in time: "Papa, where does the darkness come from?"

Don't tell her or any of the children what you know is true. You've been there already. It's that place you'd be without them.

Acknowledgments

"Amazon," "Forests," Monarch," "Quiet," and "Yoga" were first published in *The Georgia Review.*

For editorial advice, the authors thank the members of Christopher Schaberg's nonfiction writing course; and for their broadsides and books, the authors thank Karoline Schleh and the members of her letterpress and bookbinding courses. A special thanks to Ayana Cormier who did a final review of the text.

Christopher Schaberg and Mark Yakich divide their time between St. Louis and New Orleans.

Other titles available from
RedFlagPoetry.com

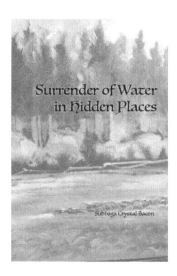

RedFlagPoetry.com or @redflagpoetry

Made in the USA
Columbia, SC
09 March 2024

32333841R00074